Wisdom for Children

JOHN MAGEE

First edition

ISBN: 979-8-47-625130-9

This book was professionally typeset on Reedsy.
Find out more at reedsy.com

To Louise, Adam and Michael.

"Children are not a distraction from more important work. They are the most important work."

C S Lewis

Contents

Preface

I hope I find you well.

This book is a collection of stories created from much loved phrases which have helped generations of children to better understand the world around them.

The phrases have been applied to modern characters and settings which every child can relate to.

Children not only need intelligence; they also require wisdom to better develop the ability to foresee the consequences of their actions as well as react constructively to the actions of others.

Helping a child to develop the capacity of judging matters relating to life and conduct themselves with compassion and understanding is a priceless gift that will be of enormous benefit to both them personally and society in general.

We need more wisdom in the world.

John Magee.

1

Two wrongs do not make a right.

Layla and Sarah were having dinner at Layla's house. They often had dinner together as they were best friends.

After the meal Layla's mum asked the girls if they would like dessert.

"Yes please!" they both shouted excitedly.

"OK" said Layla's mum. "There are some ice lollies in the fridge. You may take one each."

Layla and Sarah raced to the fridge and Layla opened the door.

"Oh!" she groaned. "There is only one lolly left." Then, before she could say or do anything more, Sarah reached around her and snatched the lolly from the fridge.

"I'm your guest so I should have it!" Sarah said boldly while taking the wrapper off the lolly.

Layla felt very sad and very angry as she watched Sarah greedily licking the lolly.

Suddenly the girls heard a loud knocking at the front door. Layla opened it to find Sarah's big sister Charlie smiling at her, "Hi Layla, Is Sarah there? Mum has said she needs to come home now as we are going to visit our Gran."

Sarah raced past Layla. "Bye, Layla" she shouted as she ran out the door with the iced lolly in her hand. "I'll see you tomorrow!"

Layla slowly closed the front door and went into the living room where her dad was reading the news on his tablet. She sat down quietly and thought about Sarah and the lolly.

"Next time Sarah comes for dinner dad just give me a lolly for dessert and not Sarah."

Her dad looked up from his tablet, "Does Sarah not like the lollies we buy?"

"No. She likes the lollies too much!" Layla exclaimed.

"I don't understand Layla. How can someone like lollies too much?" asked her dad, who was now very confused.

Layla didn't like feeling angry with her friend but she was also upset at how Sarah had behaved. It felt like there were too many emotions inside her all at once. She began to cry.

Her dad got up from the chair where he had been sitting then sat down beside Layla on the sofa. He gently wrapped his arms around her, "Why don't you tell me what has happened" he asked softly.

Layla told him the full story. When she had finished her dad sat back in the sofa and thought carefully.

"Two wrongs do not make a right" her father announced.

"What do you mean?" Layla asked confused.

"What Sarah did was wrong and she should not have behaved that way; but if you do the same thing you will be wrong too. It is better to do the right thing and help your friend to understand how they should behave in future by your example." her dad explained. "Don't worry." he said, "I have an idea."

The next day Sarah came to Layla's house and her dad offered both girls a chocolate lolly. "Yes please!" they both answered at the same time.

He went to the fridge, opened the door and pretended to be surprised "Oh!" he said. "There is only one chocolate lolly left. I understand that you had the last lolly yesterday Sarah so this one must be just for Layla today."

Layla quickly spoke up "No dad. It's not right for me to eat a whole lolly and Sarah not to have any. It is much better if we share the lolly."

"Quite right Layla" her dad said proudly. He then carefully cut the lolly into half and placed equal amounts into two bowls for the girls to eat.

After the girls finished their treat Sarah turned to Layla, "I'm so sorry Layla. I was not a good friend to you yesterday when I took the whole lolly and left you with none. You could have done the same thing today but you didn't."

Layla smiled at her friend before saying "someone very clever told me that two wrongs do not make a right."

From that day on the two friends always shared and their friendship became stronger than ever before.

2

The best things in life are free.

Liam was feeling sad. On the internet he saw people with lots of money. They lived in huge houses and owned expensive cars. They seemed to spend their time flying around the world in private jets, eating lovely food and lying on beaches.

It wasn't fair.

Why could he and his family not have that too?

It certainly wasn't because his parents didn't work hard; they were the hardest working people he knew. Liam loved them both more than anything and knew that they were doing everything they could to make a happy home for him and his new baby sister Mary.

But the harder he tried to put the thoughts of all the rich people to the back of his mind the sadder he felt.

There was one person he could talk to. His Gran.

Liam's Gran was always able to explain things in a way that he understood. She knew how to make him feel better whatever the problem.

The next day was Wednesday and Liam always had dinner at his Gran's on that day.

His mum and dad both had to work late that day and so his Gran would look after him and Mary until their dad picked them up at 6 o'clock.

He loved the Wednesday night dinners with his Gran.

The next day Liam sat at his Grans kitchen table. No sooner had she set the lovely bowl of freshly home made soup in front of him than Liam began telling her that he wished his family were richer and how he felt life was so unfair.

Gran sat forward in her chair and listened carefully to his every word. When she was sure he had finished saying everything he wanted to say, his Gran smiled gently and sat back in her chair.

Liam hardly dared to breathe as he waited for his Gran to speak.

"Liam, I am going to tell you something very important. It is so important I would even say anyone who does not know this cannot have a truly happy life."

Liam was now the one listening carefully to every word. He leaned forward in his chair.

Gran also leaned forward in her chair at the same time so that their faces were almost touching.

Slowly and carefully she whispered, "The best things in life are free."

She then sat back once again and looked at him closely.

"The best things are not free Gran, they cost a lot of money!" Liam protested.

"Then you are not thinking of the best things Liam. Things that are truly important and which bring lasting happiness" his Gran said softly.

"Love within your family. Good health. Friends to share laughter with. These are examples of the very best things in life and yet they are all free."

Liam had never thought about things like love, health and friends in that way. They had always been there for him as long as he could remember. He realised that no amount of money in the world could take their place.

The very best things in life were free and he was lucky to already have them.

Liam would continue to see people with big houses, sporty cars and fancy possessions on the internet but he no longer was jealous of them. He knew that his family, friends and health made him as rich as anyone could possibly be.

3

Better to be safe than sorry.

Alex and Adam are best friends. There is nothing they like better than riding their bikes together in the park. They are both very good at riding their bikes now but when they were learning how to ride they fell off... a lot.

One day Adam called at Alex's house on his bike. The friends had agreed to go to the park. Adam, as always, was wearing his helmet.

On this particular day Alex came out of his house without a helmet and jumped onto his bike.

"Where is your helmet Alex?" Adam asked his friend.

"It's upstairs but I don't need it any more. I know how to ride my bike and I never fall off now." Alex replied.

Adam was worried for his friend "Alex please get your helmet."

Alex thought his friend was being boring and going into his house to get his helmet would be a waste of time.

But Adam being the good friend he was, insisted that Alex wear his helmet to be safe or he would not go to the park with him.

"Better to be safe than sorry." Adam told Alex.

Adam was telling his friend that you should always do things that will keep you safe even if you think that nothing bad will happen.

Alex knew his friend was only making sure he was safe. He smiled and ran inside his house.

A short time later he reappeared wearing his helmet.

The two friends chatted happily as they cycled the short distance to the park. They then laughed together as they sped across the grass.

Suddenly a ball appeared from nowhere striking the front wheel of Alex's bike. The ball stopped the front wheel from turning and Alex shot over the handlebars of his bike.

He flew through the air and went head first into a nearby tree.

Alex was shaken but unhurt as his helmet had done its job by protecting his head.

Alex took off his helmet and looked at the huge crack.

"Thanks Adam. You were right. It's definitely better to be safe than sorry!"

4

Every dog has its day.

Freddie is absolutely mad about football. It is his favourite sport in the whole world and he likes to play whenever and wherever he can. When he is not playing football he is thinking about it.

One day there was a summer festival being held in the town where Freddie lived. There was a big parade with marching bands and lots of colourful stalls selling everything you could imagine. People could choose face painting, balloons made into shapes; as well as food and drink of every kind. The town was full of wonderful colours, sounds and smells.

Freddie however was only interested in one thing and he asked his mum if they could go straight to it.

This stall had a huge painted sign that read in large print "BEAT THE GOALIE." Below this main sign was a smaller sign, "Score three goals and win a prize."

Freddie's mum paid the person in charge of the stall and Freddie was handed a football. "Good luck young fella!" smiled the stall owner as he led Freddie to the penalty spot.

The goal suddenly looked very small to Freddie. The goalkeeper was huge and dressed in a green top, shorts and socks. Freddie had never seen anyone with hands so large.

He carefully placed the ball on the painted white spot on the grass.

A crowd had gathered to watch and began to cheer for Freddie.

Freddie carefully took aim and ran towards the ball. He kicked it with all his might to the left of the goalkeeper...

GOAL!!! The crowd cheered and applauded.

The goalkeeper picked the ball up from inside his net and threw it back to Freddie.

Once again he placed It carefully on the spot and took a few steps back. The goalkeeper moved a little to his left. This time however Freddie shot low and to the right.

GOAL!!! The crowd roared.

That was two goals out of two shots. Freddie had one shot left and if he scored a third time then he would win a prize.

The goalkeeper returned the ball to Freddie and then began jumping up and down on his line while waving his arms in order to make the goal seem even smaller.

Freddie began feeling a little nervous as he stood over the ball ready to take the third and last penalty. Should he go left or right this time? He wondered to himself.

Neither! This time he would kick the ball hard and high down the middle of the goal hoping that the goalkeeper would dive to his left or right.

Freddie took several deep breaths and then ran towards the ball. His foot made perfect contact and the ball shot forwards right in the middle of the goal as he had wished. Just as he kicked the ball Freddie also saw the goalkeeper dive to his left. The goalkeeper looked back in horror as the ball thundered towards the middle of the empty net with no hope of him stopping it.

Freddie spun around in triumph and waited for the cheers of the crowd but instead he heard...

KERRRAAAANG!!!

The ball had smashed against the crossbar while the goalkeeper lay helplessly on the ground.

The crowd couldn't believe it. A huge "Ooooooh!" echoed around.

Freddie had missed and his chance of winning a prize was gone.

The goalkeeper came forward and smiled kindly at Freddie, "Great effort lad. It was really bad luck to hit the crossbar but always remember...every dog has its day."

Freddie was confused. What did the man mean? Dogs can't take penalties!

Freddie's mum saw his confusion, "It simply means that although things don't go the way you want today, they will another day. Never give up and keep trying."

The goalkeeper proved correct. In the years that followed there were days when Freddie would win and days that he would lose.

Freddie never let the days he lost make him too sad because he knew that if he kept trying and never gave up he would have winning days too.

5

Many hands make light work.

James, David, William and John were great friends. They had met on their very first day of school and became best friends straight away.

One day they were playing in David's house when his mother came into the room, "My goodness, just look at all the toys over the floor!" she cried "this will all need to be tidied up before anyone goes home."

She then left the boys to do as she had asked.

"I'm not doing it as I wasn't the last to play with them." John said quickly.

"Well, I'm not doing it as I didn't get them out." added James.

"I'm not doing it as I only played with one of them." said William.

"Well I'm certainly not doing it all on my own!" shouted David.

After several minutes of arguing and no toys being tidied, David's mum returned.

She was not happy. Not happy at all.

"Why have you not tidied the room as I asked?"

At this point it was getting very near to each of their dinner times.

James, William and John said there was now not enough time to tidy the entire room.

"Many hands make light work" David's mum told them.

"What does that mean mum?" asked David.

"It means that any work is easier for everyone if it is shared" she replied.

The four friends began lifting and putting away the toys together and sure enough, within a very short period of time the room had been completely tidied.

What would have taken one of them a long time had been completed by all four friends quickly and easily by sharing and working together.

6

Do not judge a book by its cover.

One Sunday Sophie was enjoying some exercise with her father. It was a crisp autumn morning and the two often walked along the river path in the park nearby.

In the distance Sophie saw a boy walking towards them. Even though he was still far away she could see his face and clothes were very muddy.

As the boy got nearer he raised his hand to wave hello and Sophie could see that it too was covered in mud.

"Look at that boy Daddy. He must not wash and be very naughty. I would not want to be friends with someone like that." Sophie whispered to her father.

As the boy got even closer Sophie's dad recognized him as the son of someone he worked with. "Goodness Mohamed!" he said "What on earth has happened to you?"

Mohamed had visited his father at work many times and so he recognised Sophie's dad "Hello Mr. Stone." he replied very politely. "I saw a girl with a little puppy stuck in the mud. I was helping her to get her puppy out. It was very slippery and I'm covered in mud but thankfully we both managed to do it and the puppy is OK."

"Can I do anything Mohamed? Do you want us to walk back home with you?" Asked Sophie's dad.

"No thank you Mr. Stone, I just live there!" laughed Mohamed pointing to a nearby house.

"Well done for helping the little girl and the puppy." Sophie's dad said to Mohamed as he waved goodbye.

Sophie was very quiet as she continued the walk with her father.

After a few minutes she finally spoke, "I was wrong about that boy daddy. He is very kind and I would like to be friends with him."

Sophie's father smiled and gave her a big hug "You have learned an important lesson today Sophie. Do not judge a book by its cover."

"What do you mean?" Sophie asked.

"I simply mean that how a person looks does not tell you if they are a good or bad person."

The next day Sophie's dad spoke to Mohamed's father and they arranged a time to bring the children to the nearby park.

Sophie and Mohamed had a wonderful day playing together and soon became great friends.

7

Horses for courses.

Henry loves his older brother Thomas. To look at them however, you would never guess they are brothers. Thomas is tall, strong and very good at every type of sport you can imagine. Henry is small and does not have the same levels of strength and energy as Thomas.

Henry had tried running, football, swimming, tennis, golf, hockey, rugby, basketball and even judo but he did not feel he was good at any of them .

As you can imagine this was hard for Henry when he wanted to be so much like his older brother who made every sport look easy.

One day after Henry had tried yet another sport, his parents said to him "Never worry Henry. There are horses for courses."

Henry asked his parents what they meant.

They said it simply means different people are able to do different things. You just need to keep trying different things and one day you will find the thing that suits you best.

Henry thought if he continued to try different sports that one day he would find one that he was very good at but it seemed to Henry that after each new sport he tried, this was not true for him.

Then something happened completely by chance that proved to Henry his parents were right all along. He had simply been looking in the wrong place for the thing he was good at.

You see Henry thought because his brother Thomas was good at sports, he should be good at a sport as well. He never considered the thing he would be good at may have nothing to do with a sport of any kind. He was looking in the wrong place.

His discovery began one evening just after dinner. Henry and Thomas were doing their homework in their bedrooms. Henry always finished his homework quickly as he really enjoyed it, especially mathematics.

Henry had always loved numbers for as long as he could remember. In fact he loved them so much he just assumed everyone else must love them too.

On this particular evening Henry was passing the open door of his brothers bedroom when he heard a shout coming from inside. Henry peeked in to find his brother with his head in his hands and a large book lying open in front of him.

"Is everything OK Thomas?" Henry asked.

"No." said Thomas sadly. "I just cannot understand how to do these numbers."

Henry was not sure what to say at first. His brother Thomas was having difficulty with numbers of all things.

"Let me take a look" said Henry helpfully.

Henry patiently and thoughtfully helped his brother to understand the numbers.

It became very clear that Henry was not only good at understanding numbers, he was also a wonderful teacher because of his patience.

Henry discovered his talent was numbers and teaching.

In the years that followed he became a brilliant maths teacher and helped thousands of boys and girls to understand their numbers.

8

A bad worker blames the tools.

Harry and Jack were playing together in the front room of Harry's house.

The two friends loved playing together. Sometimes to make things even more fun they would have challenges.

"What challenge shall we have today?" Harry asked his friend.

"What about building the tallest tower out of blocks?" Jack suggested.

"Fantastic idea!" said Harry. "Let's see how high each of us can build our tower!".

The friends shared the wooden building blocks out equally so each of them had exactly 10.

Jack was slow and careful. He began by selecting a part of the floor that was very even and had no bumps.

Harry however was fast and not nearly so careful. He placed the first block of his tower on the rug he was sitting on. It was very uneven.

Jack placed each of his bricks on top of the other slowly and carefully. He made sure that each block was steady on the one underneath before he placed the next on top. Slowly but surely he built his tower until it proudly stood 10 blocks high. Success!

Harry had wanted to get his tower made first. He rushed and placed his block on the very edge of the first. He did the same with the next block and then the next.

CRASH!

Harry's tower fell down as he tried to place his fifth block.

Harry looked at Jack's tall tower of 10 blocks and shouted "My blocks don't work! Your blocks are better than mine!"

Jack laughed at his friend and said "A bad worker blames the tools!"

Harry did not know what Jack was saying.

So his friend explained, "Your blocks are exactly the same as mine Harry. They didn't make your tower fell over, you did. You started your tower on a bumpy rug and didn't put each block on top of the other carefully."

Jack helped Harry to move his blocks to a part of the floor that was perfectly flat and even. Harry then carefully began placing each of his blocks just as Jack had done until he too had built a tall tower of 10 blocks.

The two friends then laughed as they knocked each of their towers over!

9

Look before you leap.

Nia was given a very special surprise present on her birthday when she visited her grandpa. He had covered her eyes with his hands and led her into the back garden before taking his hands quickly away.

Nia opened her eyes and blinked in the sunlight. There before her was the most beautiful tree-house. It had a ladder leading up to the entrance.

Nia could not have been happier at that moment.

"Oh grandpa thank you, thank you, thank you!" she screamed as she threw her arms around him and gave him the biggest hug.

Nia then raced over to her new tree-house and quickly climbed the steps. It was just wonderful. It had a little window from which she could see her grandpa sitting in his favourite chair. The roof and floor of the tree-house was made of wood and her Grandpa had made it just the right size for Nia and two friends.

"Its perfect grandpa!" Nia called through the window to her grandpa who was a short distance away in the garden raking leaves. "I am going to fill it with lots of nice things and invite my friends" Nia said excitedly.

Her grandpa smiled and said "OK Nia but always look before you leap."

Nia was not sure what her grandpa meant but she was too excited with her plans for the tree-house to ask him to explain. She rushed past him into his house and straight to the bedroom where she stayed when having sleepovers. Nia began taking books, chairs, her toy tea set, papers and pens, blankets, pillows and games across the garden and pushing each through the entrance of the tree-house.

After what must have been her twentieth journey across the garden she had finally finished.

"Grandpa can I go next door to invite Hanna and Cadence into my tree-house?" Nia asked.

"Yes you can but before you do..." Her Grandpa could say nothing more as Nia had already raced out of the garden to get her friends.

Several minutes later Nia arrived back with both friends. "Quick" Nia shouted excitedly, "lets go inside."

Nia scrambled up the ladder and into the tree-house first but was puzzled when, instead of joining her inside, her friends stopped at the entrance.

"What are you doing?" Nia asked her friends "Come in, come in!"

"We can't." Her friends replied. "There is no room for us!"

Nia's grandpa who had been watching and listening let out a great laugh, "I tried telling you to look before you leap. It means that before you do something you should think about it carefully. If you had stopped and thought you would have realized that moving all those things into the tree-house did not leave any room for your friends to join you inside."

Nia, Hanna and Cadence all began laughing!

The three friends and grandpa helped to move enough things out of the tree-house so there was plenty of room to play inside.

Nia and her friends would enjoy many, many happy times in the tree-house her Grandpa had built.

10

Beauty is in the eye of the beholder.

Michael, Oliver, Jessica and Poppy were very excited. They are visiting a special place called an art gallery. This is a place where artists who have painted pictures can display them for other people to enjoy.

The four friends entered a large room in the art gallery where lots and lots of pictures hung on the walls for them to see.

The first painting they looked at was of a brown horse galloping across a green field.

Michael, Jessica and Poppy thought the painting was beautiful.

Oliver however did not. He did not like it at all.

He disliked it so much, he thought his friends were wrong to find it beautiful.

"It's just a horse." he stated. "You can't find a horse running in a field beautiful!"

Michael simply said to Oliver "Beauty is in the eye of the beholder." and the three other friends then moved to look at the next painting.

Oliver caught up with his friends and said to Michael "I don't know what you mean!"

Michael explained to his friend, "It means we are all different and we can like different things. Just because you do not like the painting does not mean Poppy, Jessica and I cannot."

As the friends went through the art gallery and looked at many more paintings, it became clear to Oliver that his friend was correct. Each of the friends liked different paintings. It did not mean that anyone was right or wrong. It just demonstrated that each of us can see things we like when others do not.

It is makes each and every person special and the world such an interesting place.

11

Mighty oaks from little acorns grow.

Charlotte was incredibly proud of her mum. She was a professional footballer and played for one of the top teams in the country.

In fact her mum was the leading goalscorer. She had amazing skill, speed and strength making her able to often score spectacular goals.

After her latest game Charlotte's mum returned home; but instead of being greeted by her daughter in celebration as usual, she found her daughter sitting sadly at the foot of the stairs.

"Oh dear" her mum said. "Have you done something wrong? Has Daddy asked you to sit on the naughty step?"

"No!" Charlotte said quickly.

"Then what is it? Why the sad face?" her mum asked worriedly.

"You wouldn't understand." Charlotte said sadly.

"Try me." said her mum, and she sat beside her daughter on the stairs.

Charlotte thought for a few moments.

In the past Charlotte told her mum everything. Her mum had always been able to help but Charlotte was sure this time her mum couldn't. Charlotte was actually worried her mum would think she was being silly.

Charlotte took a deep breath and spoke very softly.

"You are big, strong and fast," Charlotte began, "I am so small, slow and weak" she continued. "I can't play football the way you can and I never will."

Charlotte's mum gently cradled her in her arms and whispered softly in her ear "Mighty oaks from little acorns grow".

Charlotte looked at her mum hoping for an explanation but instead her mum shouted cheerily "follow me!" and she darted upstairs.

Charlotte chased after her mum who had disappeared out of sight.

"Mum, where are you?" Charlotte called.

"No need to shout. I'm just here" came her mothers voice from the spare bedroom. Charlotte entered the room but still could not see her mum. Then up popped her mums head suddenly from where she had been searching under the bed.

"Here it is!" her mum said happily, and in her hands was what seemed to be a thick book.

"What book is that?" Charlotte asked her mum.

"Oh, its not a book, its a very old photo album. I want you to look at some photographs with me." Her mum said as she sat on the bed and opened the heavy red cover.

Charlotte joined her mother on the bed and stared at a photograph of the smallest little girl she had ever seen. The little girl in the photograph was probably the same age as Charlotte but she looked younger because she was so small. She looked as if a gust of wind would blow her away.

"Who is that tiny little girl?" Charlotte asked.

"That tiny, little girl…" said her mother proudly "…was me."

Charlotte simply couldn't believe it. Then she looked more closely at the little girl in the photograph. Charlotte looked past the thin legs and arms and focused on the face. She could see the unmistakable kind and gentle eyes of her mum.

"Mighty oaks from little acorns grow" her mother said again. "Over time you will grow bigger and stronger just as I did. Plants must have sunlight and water to grow; children need fruit, vegetables and exercise."

Charlotte understood. Once again her mum had helped and made her feel much better.

Charlotte exercised and ate healthily; and every year she grew bigger and stronger.

Just as every child does.

12

Actions speak louder than words.

Isla and Emily live next to each other. It is the summer holidays and the weather is warm and sunny.

Emily has a brilliant idea, "why don't we have a picnic in my garden tomorrow?"

Isla quickly agrees and the two friends talk excitedly about what they will need for the picnic.

Emily tells Isla that she will make buns. Isla said she will make iced lollies and bring fruit.

The two friends then agree to meet in Emily's garden the next day at 1 o'clock for their picnic.

Emily goes into her house but instead of beginning to prepare the buns she promised to bring the next day, she begins watching television and soon forgets all about the picnic.

Isla however began making the iced lollies she had promised as soon as she returned home. She also picked lots of lovely fruit and washed it so all was ready for the picnic.

The next day arrives and exactly at 1 o'clock Isla calls at Emily's home, just as the friends had agreed the day before.

When Emily sees the lollies and fruit her friend has brought for the picnic she tells her, "Sorry Isla. I didn't make the buns for the picnic but I promise that I will make them for tomorrow."

Isla is cross and tells her friend, "Actions speak louder than words."

"What do you mean Isla?" Emily asks.

Isla explains, "it is easy to say you will do something but it is not the same thing as actually doing it."

Emily knows she is wrong and apologises to Isla.

Isla can see her friend is very sorry and gives her a big smile saying "Let's have the iced lollies and fruit!"

The two friends have a wonderful afternoon enjoying the food Isla has brought.

The next day Emily does exactly what she promised she would do and calls at Isla's house with freshly made buns for them both to enjoy.

About the Author

John lives with Louise and their two sons in Omagh, N. Ireland. He spent 30 years as an international trade consultant travelling the world; meeting people from many cultures and backgrounds. He witnessed wisdom within people that made their own life better and also the lives of those around them. John is committed to encouraging and helping future generations communicate more wisely with one another to live truly happy lives.

Printed in Great Britain
by Amazon